# Little Bo Peep's Missing Sheep

# Crabtree Publishing Company

www.crabtreebooks.com
1-800-387-7650

PMB 59051, 350 Fifth Ave.   616 Welland Ave.
59th Floor,   St. Catharines, ON
New York, NY 10118   L2M 5V6

Published by Crabtree Publishing in 2013

**Series editor:** Louise John
**Editors:** Katie Powell, Kathy Middleton
**Notes to adults:** Reagan Miller
**Cover design:** Paul Cherrill
**Design:** D.R.ink
**Consultant:** Shirley Bickler
**Production coordinator and**
   **Prepress technician:** Margaret Amy Salter
**Print coordinator:** Katherine Berti

Text © Alan Durant 2009
Illustration © Leah-Ellen Heming 2009

First published in 2009 by Wayland (A division of Hachette Children's Books)

Printed in Hong Kong/ 092012/BK20120629

**Library and Archives Canada Cataloguing in Publication**

CIP available at Library and Archives Canada

**Library of Congress Cataloging-in-Publication Data**

CIP available at Library of Congress

# Little Bo Peep's Missing Sheep

**Written by Alan Durant**
**Illustrated by Leah-Ellen Heming**

## Crabtree Publishing Company
www.crabtreebooks.com

One snowy winter's morning, Little
Bo Peep looked out of her window—and
got a big shock. Her sheep were gone!

She picked up her crook and ran out into the meadow. No sheep! Where could they be? And where was her friend Little Boy Blue, who was supposed to be looking after them?

"Sheep, sheep!" she called.
"Little Boy Blue, where are you?"
Little Bo Peep was puzzled.

Then she saw hoofprints in the snow. "They'll lead me to my sheep," she thought. So, off she went following them.

Little Bo Peep hadn't gone very
far when she met Mary.
"Have you seen my sheep?"
asked Little Bo Peep.

Mary shook her head. "Have you seen my
little lamb?" she asked. "He was following
me to school, and when I looked around
he was gone. What am I going to do?"
she wailed.

Mary started to cry.
"There, there," soothed Bo Peep.
"We'll find him. He's probably with
my sheep. Come with me."

So Little Bo Peep and Mary
followed the trail of hoofprints
through the snow.

They went round and round a mulberry bush, but there was no sign of any sheep—just children pretending to wash their hands.

"Have you seen my sheep?"
asked Little Bo Peep.
"And my lamb?" added Mary.

"No," said the children, "but this is the
way we go to school, go to school, go
to school," they sang. And off they went.

Little Bo Peep and Mary carried on following the hoofprints through the snow, until they came to the house that Jack built.

Little Bo Peep knocked. "Yes?" asked Jack.

"I've lost my sheep," said Little Bo Peep.
"And I've lost my lamb," added Mary.
"Have you seen them?" they asked.

"Come in and have a look," said Jack.
"It's my wedding party, you know."

It was very crowded in Jack's house.
There was a farmer with a bag of corn,
a crowing cock, a priest all shaven
and shorn, a maiden all forlorn,
a cow with a crumpled horn, and
a dog and a cat chasing a rat.

But no sheep. Yet, there, at the back
door, were the hoofprints again!

The hoofprints led to Mary's garden. "Oh, dear," said Little Bo Peep. Mary's garden was in a terrible state. There were silver bells and cockle shells all over the place.

"Look at my pretty maids," sighed Mary.
"I planted them all in a row. What a mess
they're in!"

At that moment they heard a noise.
Snip, snip, snip. It was coming from
behind the garden wall.

Snip, snip, snip.

Little Bo Peep and Mary went
to investigate.
"Oh, no!" they cried.

There was Tom, the piper's son, snipping
the woolly coat of a sheep with a pair
of scissors!

"Stop, thief!" Little Bo Peep commanded.
"What are you doing to my sheep?"
"I'm filling up these three bags with wool,"
said Tom. "One for the master, and one for
the dame, and one for the little boy who
lives down the lane."

He grinned. "That's me!"

"But you can't do that," wailed Little Bo Peep. "Those sheep belong to me." "And that little lamb belongs to me!" added Mary.

Tom stuck out his tongue. "Prove it!" he taunted.

Little Bo Peep and Mary looked
at each other. How could they prove the
sheep and the lamb belonged to them?

Suddenly...TAN-TARAN-TARA!
It was Little Boy Blue. He had just woken
up from his sleep under a haystack, and
he was blowing his horn!

At once the sheep turned and ran
for home. The little lamb leaped up
into Mary's arms.

"I think that proves it," said Little Bo Peep.

"Nuts!" said Tom with a scowl. "I would have gotten a good price for those sheep at the market."

"Excuse me," squealed a little voice. "Did you say market?" It was a small pig. "I'm on my way there, you see, but I'm rather lost."

Tom's scowl turned to a grin once more. "I'll take you," he laughed, and he picked up the pig and away he ran!

"That naughty boy," sighed
Little Bo Peep.
"At least you got your sheep
back," said Mary.

"And you got your little lamb,"
said Little Bo Peep.
"Baa," bleated the little lamb happily.

Then they followed the sheep home...
bringing this tale behind them!

# Notes for adults

Tadpoles: **Nursery Crimes** are structured for transitional and early fluent readers. The books may also be used for read-alouds or shared reading with younger children.

Tadpoles: **Nursery Crimes** are intended for children who are familiar with nursery rhyme characters and themes, but can also be enjoyed by anyone. Each story can be compared with the traditional rhyme, or appreciated for its own unique twist.

## IF YOU ARE READING THIS BOOK WITH A CHILD, HERE ARE A FEW SUGGESTIONS:

1. Make reading fun! Choose a time to read when you and the child are relaxed and have time to share the story.

2. Before reading, invite the child to preview the book. The child can read the title, look at the illustrations, skim through the text, and make predictions as to what will happen in the story. This activity stimulates curiosity and promotes critical thinking skills.

3. During reading, encourage the child to monitor his or her understanding by asking questions to draw conclusions, making connections, and using context clues to understand unfamiliar words.

4. After reading, ask the child to review his or her predictions. Were they correct? Discuss different parts of the story, including main characters, setting, main events, the problem and solution. Challenge the child to retell the story in his or her own words to enhance comprehension.

5. Give praise! Children learn best in a positive environment.

## VISIT THE LIBRARY AND CHECK OUT THESE RELATED NURSERY RHYMES AND CHILDREN'S SONGS:

*Little Bo Peep*
*Little Boy Blue*
*Mary Had a Little Lamb*

*Here We Go Round the*
  *Mulberry Bush*
*The House that Jack Built*
*Mary, Mary, Quite Contrary*

*Tom, Tom, the Piper's Son*
*Baa, Baa, Black Sheep*
*To Market, To Market*

## IF YOU ENJOYED THIS BOOK, WHY NOT TRY ANOTHER TADPOLES: NURSERY CRIMES STORY?

*Humpty Dumpty's Great Fall*       978-0-7787-8028-1 RLB       978-0-7787-8039-7 PB
*Little Miss Muffet's Big Scare*   978-0-7787-8030-4 RLB       978-0-7787-8041-0 PB
*Mother Hubbard's Stolen Bone*     978-0-7787-8031-1 RLB       978-0-7787-8042-7 PB

VISIT **WWW.CRABTREEBOOKS.COM** FOR OTHER CRABTREE BOOKS.